SPIDER!

By Carrie Hyatt
Illustrated by Tatiana Kamshilina

DEDICATION

This story is dedicated to those like me who are still learning to appreciate our little arachnid friends and share our space in the world with them.

SPIDER!

NOPE!
IT'S A DADDY LONGLEGS!

HEY! THERE'S OUR SPIDER NOW. LET'S SAY GOODBYE!

ABOUT THE AUTHOR

Carrie Hyatt is a devoted wife and a mother of two. Her hobbies include reading books of all kinds and writing children's stories. Carrie loves Pizza-Thursdays with her family and teaching Sunday School. She and her husband run a chiropractic office in Oak Creek, WI.

47909313R00019

Made in the USA
Lexington, KY
13 August 2019